With thanks to God, with love to my family,
and to the children of Triple S Camp
—K. S.

To my family in Japan
—A. H.

Atheneum Books for Young Readers
An imprint of Simon & Schuster Children's
Publishing Division
1230 Avenue of the Americas
New York, New York 10020

Text copyright © 2002 by Kitoba Sunami
Illustrations copyright © 2002 by Amiko Hirao

Book design by Ann Bobco and Sonia Chaghatzbanian
The text of this book is set in Cantoria, Centaur, and Triplex.

The illustrations are rendered in pastels.

Printed in Hong Kong
10 9 8 7 6 5 4 3 2 1
Library of Congress Cataloging-in-Publication Data
Sunami, Kitoba.
How the fisherman tricked the genie : a tale within a tale within a
tale / by Kitoba Sunami ;
illustrated by Amiko Hirao.—1st ed.
p.   cm.
Summary: After releasing a captive genie from a bottle, a poor fisherman
must rely on his wits when instead of wishes, the genie promises revenge.

ISBN 0-689-83399-7
[1. Fairy tales. 2. Revenge—Fiction.]
I. Hirao, Amiko, ill. II. Title.
PZ8.S855 Dh 2002
[Fic]—dc21   00-024410

FIRST
EDITION

How the fISHERMAN tRICKED the genie

A Tale Within a Tale Within a Tale

by

Kitoba Sunami

illustrated by

Amiko Hirao

ATHENEUM BOOKS FOR YOUNG READERS
New York London Toronto Sydney Singapore

The child is young.
The day is old.
My story is waiting.
It wants to be told.

Once there was a poor fisherman who lived by the shores of the Arabian Sea. Every day, he would go down to the shining waters and cast out his nets. But, every day, it was harder and harder for him to make a living by fishing. Finally, he decided he would only cast out his net three more times, and if he did not make some truly miraculous catch, he would turn in his nets and go to beg on the streets.

The first time he cast out his net, he pulled it in empty. The second time he cast it out, it was very heavy, and hard to pull in. But, instead of fish, the only thing in the net was a giant rotting tree stump.

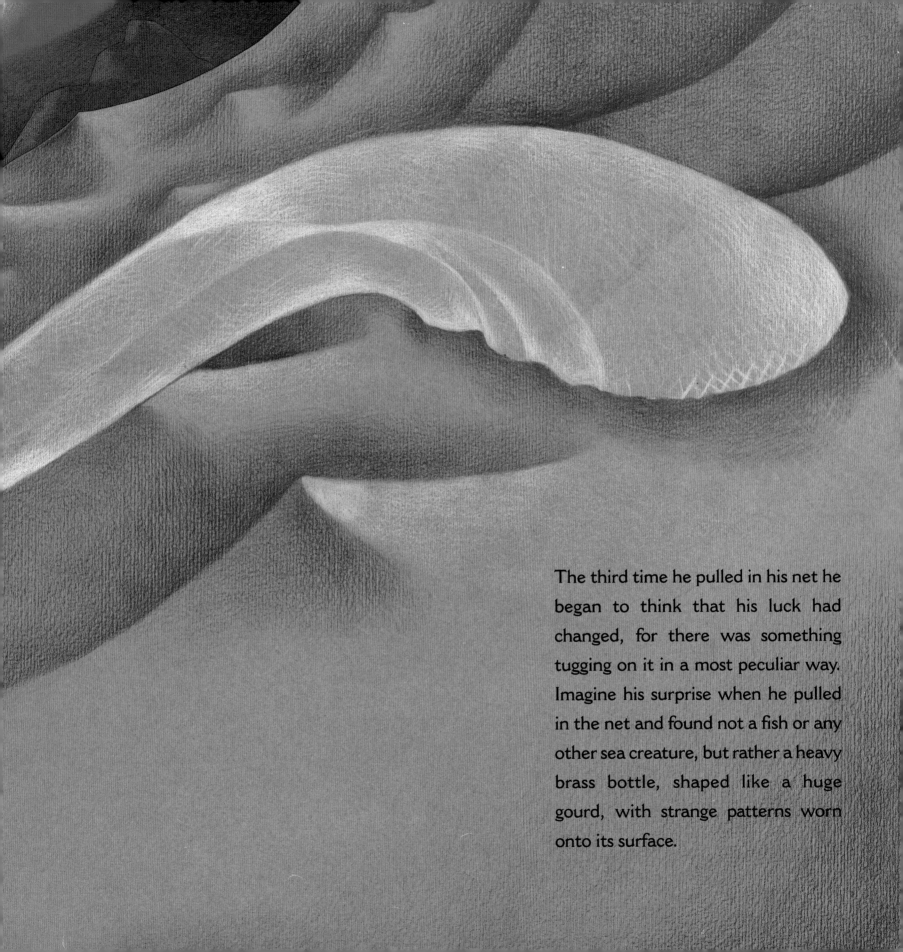

The third time he pulled in his net he began to think that his luck had changed, for there was something tugging on it in a most peculiar way. Imagine his surprise when he pulled in the net and found not a fish or any other sea creature, but rather a heavy brass bottle, shaped like a huge gourd, with strange patterns worn onto its surface.

The fisherman shook the bottle, then held it up to his ear. He noticed that the bottle was warm to the touch, and that it seemed to shake slightly in his hands. He set the bottle on the rocks and pulled gently on the stopper. There was a big WHOOSH! A huge cloud of smoke billowed out of the bottle. The smoke formed itself into an enormous genie, three times as big as a house. His skin was deep blue, his eyes were dark red, and he had a turban on his head and a sword at his waist. He looked straight at the fisherman, and in a deep booming voice shouted, "PREPARE TO DIE!"

The fisherman was surprised and frightened, and immediately began to protest.

"Wait!" he said. "Aren't you supposed to grant me three wishes?"

The genie scowled. "KNOW THIS!" he shouted. "I am one of those evil spirits who rebelled against Heaven and were defeated by King Solomon the Great. For THREE THOUSAND LONG YEARS, I have been condemned to live in this bottle!"

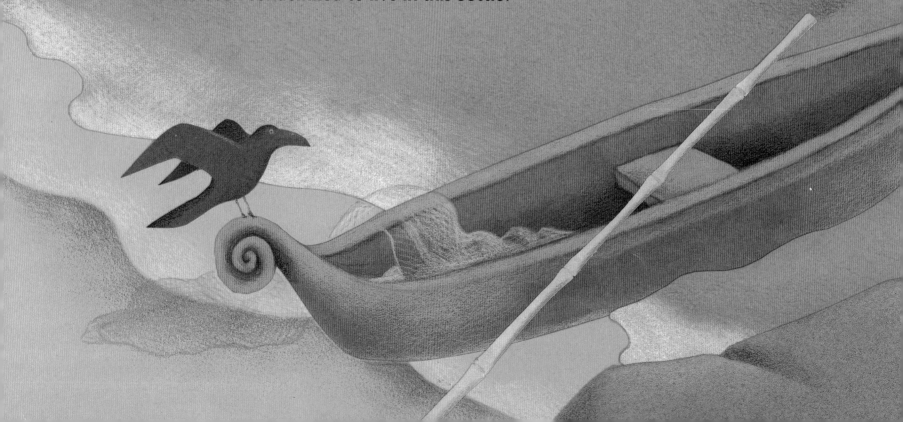

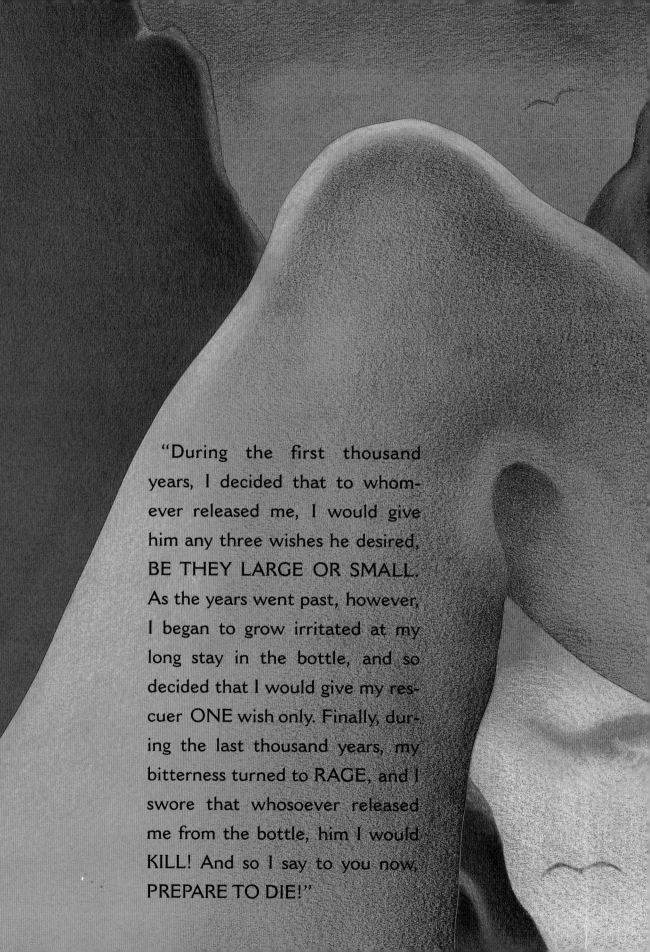

"During the first thousand years, I decided that to whomever released me, I would give him any three wishes he desired, BE THEY LARGE OR SMALL. As the years went past, however, I began to grow irritated at my long stay in the bottle, and so decided that I would give my rescuer ONE wish only. Finally, during the last thousand years, my bitterness turned to RAGE, and I swore that whosoever released me from the bottle, him I would KILL! And so I say to you now, PREPARE TO DIE!"

"Wait!" said the fisherman. "I just helped you by releasing you from the bottle."

"And I have just explained that it is THAT VERY ACT that has sealed your fate!" replied the genie.

"But," said the fisherman, "you must know that you should never repay a good deed with an evil one. For some evil will surely befall you in turn."

"DO NOT ATTEMPT TO SCARE ME!" said the genie. "WHAT CAN YOU DO TO HARM AN ALL-POWERFUL GENIE?!"

"Oh, it is not I who will punish you, but rather Heaven and Fate," replied the fisherman. "Let me tell you a story that will help explain."

And this is the story that the fisherman told the genie:

Once there was a rich and powerful king. His treasury was overflowing with gold and silver, and he had the best of everything money could buy. His wealth did him no good, however, when he caught a mysterious illness and seemed sure to die. He hired all the best doctors from five nearby kingdoms, but one by one they all failed to cure him. Finally, there came to the gates of the castle a strange little man named Dhuban the Doctor. He was short, no taller than a child, and as skinny as a bean pole. His skin was greenish, and he wore nothing but a loincloth. In the middle of his forehead, he had a tattoo that looked just like a third eye, and hung around his neck was a little leather pouch.

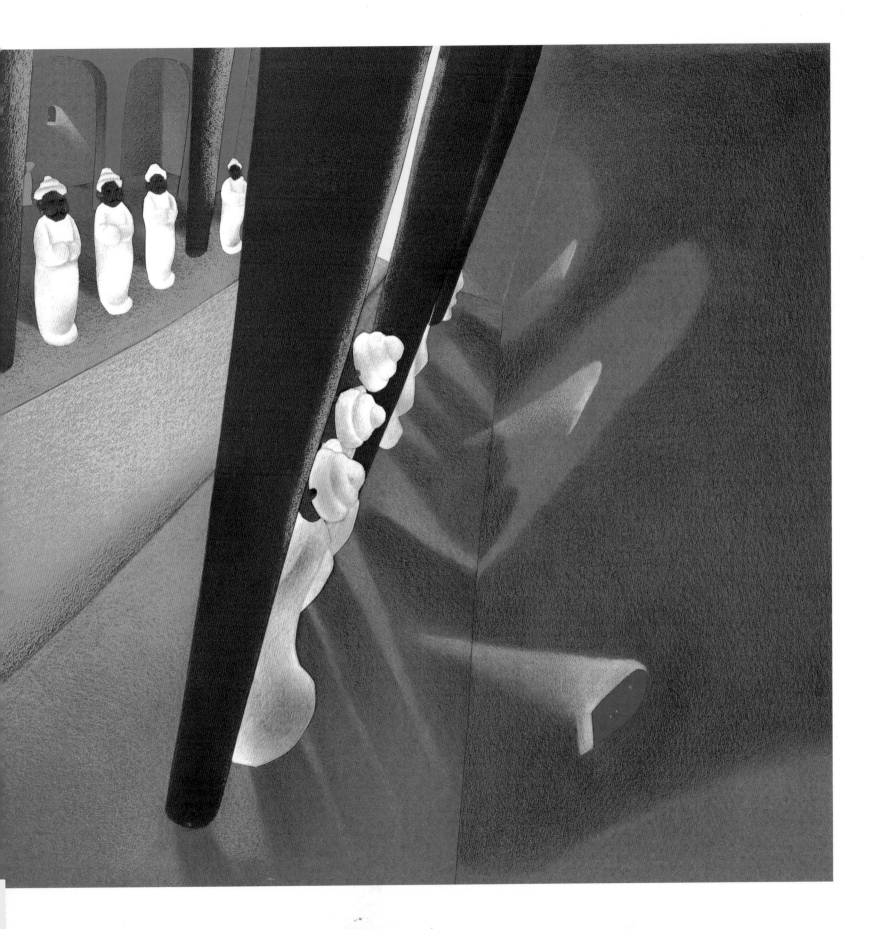

Normally, such an odd person would have never been allowed into the palace, but the king was desperate to be cured. So he let Dhuban peek at his throat and in his ears, and to poke his stomach and his chest. Finally, at length, he heard Dhuban deliver his diagnosis in a soft whispery voice.

"King," he said. "You are very ill, but there is a cure."

"Tell me what it is!" croaked the king. "I'll give you anything if you can cure me."

"King," Dhuban warned. "This cure, you may not like."

"Tell me, please!" the king begged.

"The memories of kings are short," said Dhuban. "When you are well, you will forget Dhuban and the debt you owe him."

"Never!" said the king. "I swear, as long as I live, you will always have my undying gratitude."

"Very well," said Dhuban. "Listen carefully, and omit not a single word of what I say. You must immediately go down to the foot of the palace and strip off all your clothes. Smear your body with mud from the river and run backward around the palace three times, crowing like a rooster. Then you will be cured."

The king was so afraid of death that he was willing to try even this bizarre cure. So, he went down to the palace gates and threw off his royal robes. Then, he smeared himself with mud and ran backward around the castle three times, crowing like a rooster. And the very moment he finished, he was miraculously healed.

At first, he was overjoyed. Quickly, however, his happiness faded and was replaced by bitterness. All he could think about was how humiliating his treatment had been. "That doctor made me look ridiculous," he thought. "How will my subjects ever respect me now?" Finally, he decided to restore his pride by killing the one who embarrassed him. So, he sent for Dhuban.

"Yes, King?" said Dhuban. "Do you wish to give me my reward?"

"Yes," said the king, as he chuckled to himself. "You will receive your reward. Prepare yourself . . . for death!"

"I see," said Dhuban. "Have you so quickly forgotten your promise to me? To kill one who has saved your life is a great evil."

The king laughed. "I know," he said. "But who can punish me? I am an all-powerful king!" At these words, Dhuban looked very sad.

"Who will punish you?" he said. "Heaven, and Fate."

And then he told the king the following story:

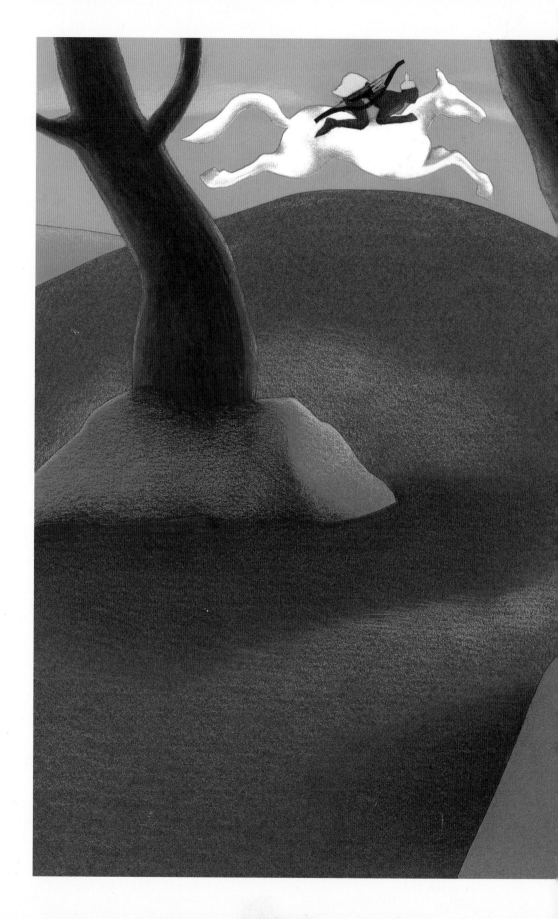

Once, King, there was a strong young prince who always had the best of everything, and never knew hunger or pain. Perhaps you were like this prince once, King.

More than anything else, this prince loved to hunt, and so, every day he would go off, deep into the enchanted forest. His mount was a great white horse, the color of fresh milk, and his companion was a faithful dog, which he had raised from a pup.

One day, as they were out riding, the prince caught sight of a most beautiful deer. It shone in the sun-light, as if made of gold.

Off they went, chasing this deer, mile after mile after mile. Once, they came close to it but suddenly it leapt into the air and sailed clear over a river blocking the path.

Then, just as the prince was about to follow, the dog bit the great white horse on the leg. It jumped straight up into the air, and, when it came down, its leg was broken.

Now there was no way the prince could catch up to the deer.

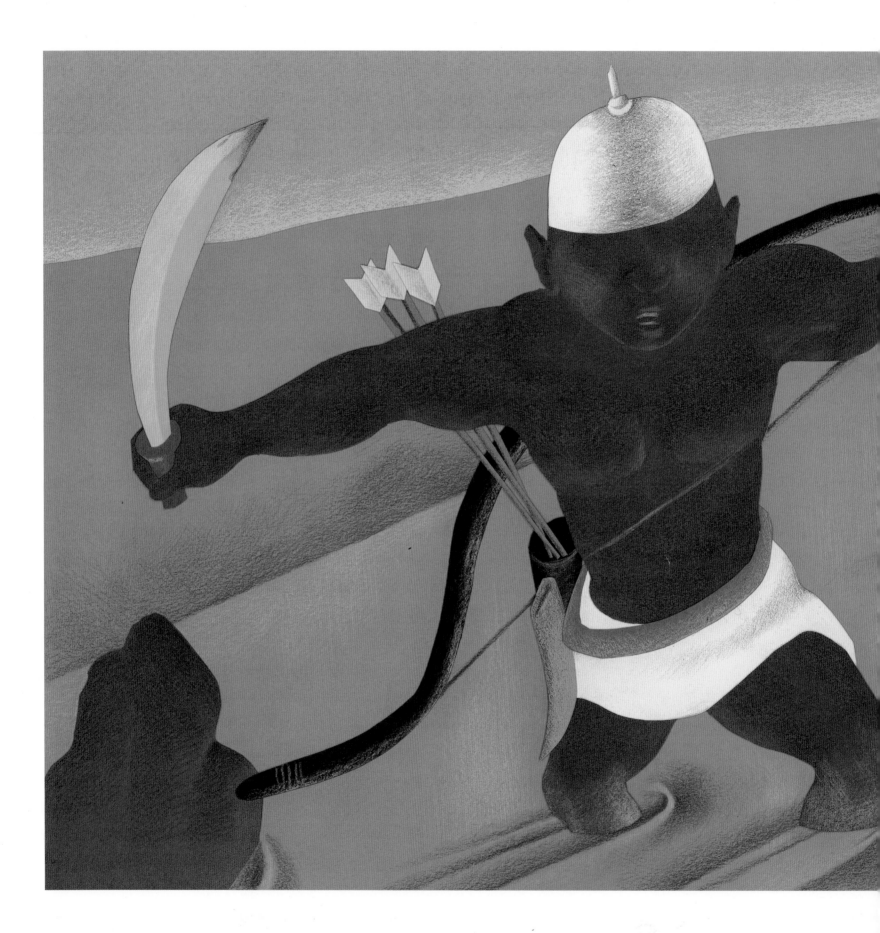

He became very angry and then did a terrible thing, King. He took his sword and killed the dog, the dog that was his best friend. Then, even though he could no longer catch the deer, he waded out into the middle of the stream.

But, as he entered the water, he suddenly felt cold and heavy. He looked down, and saw, to his horror, that his legs and feet had turned to stone. It was a cursed stream he had entered, King, a stream that turned everything it touched into cold, hard rock. Now the prince realized that the dog had only been trying to save him from this horrible fate. His last thoughts were of regret for his evil deed."

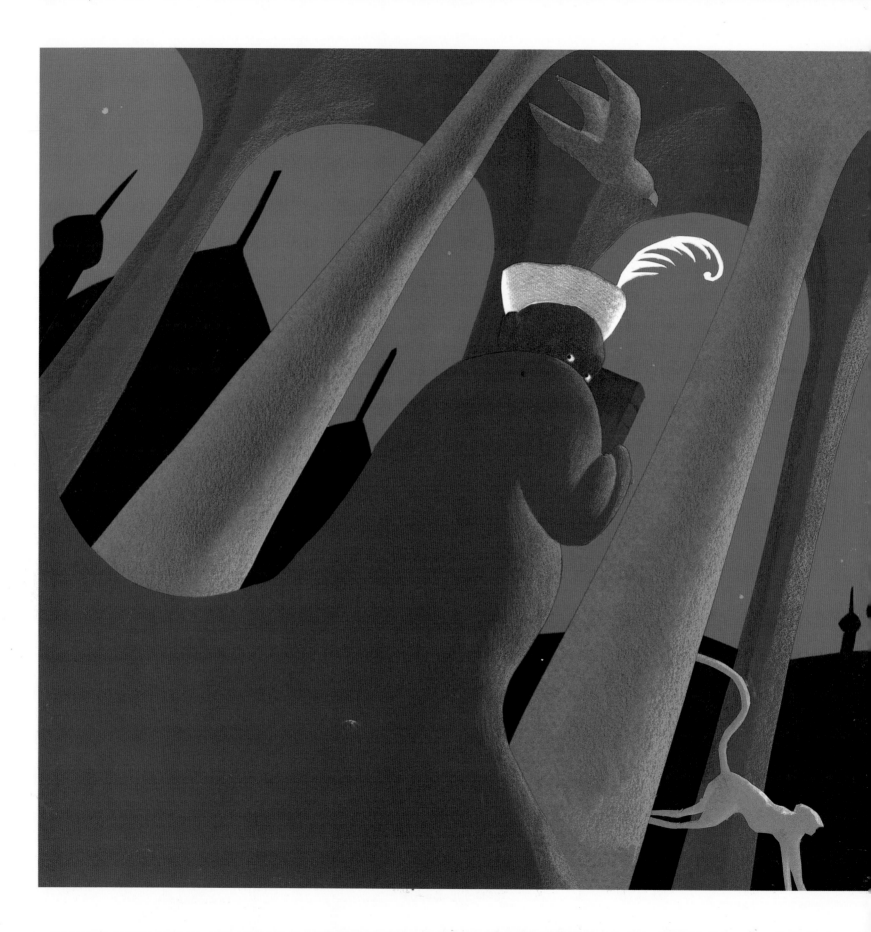

Now do you understand, King?" said Dhuban, softly.

"You can't scare me, old man," said the king.

Dhuban sighed. "Before I die," he said, "I have one last favor to ask. In my belongings, you will find a large heavy book with a red leather cover. It contains all my magic secrets, and whosoever reads it will become a powerful enchanter. Take this book and burn it, King. It must never fall into the wrong hands."

The king quickly agreed, but, as soon as Dhuban was dead, he rushed off to read the book himself.

When he opened the book to the first page he found that it was completely blank, and when he tried to open to the second page, he found that the pages were stuck together! Licking his finger to help him turn the page, he continued—but each page was blank, and stuck to the next.

On the last page was a picture of Dhuban. His three eyes seemed to burn deep into the king's soul. Underneath the picture was printed the following:

FOOLISH KING. You had one last chance to save yourself. HAD YOU BURNED THIS BOOK AS I ASKED, ALL WOULD BE WELL. But, since you are reading this now, then you have ignored my final request. If you have gotten this far into the book then you know that the pages were stuck together. PERHAPS YOU LICKED YOUR FINGER TO TURN THE PAGES? . . . Those pages were stuck together with poison!

As the king read these final words, he fell down dead.

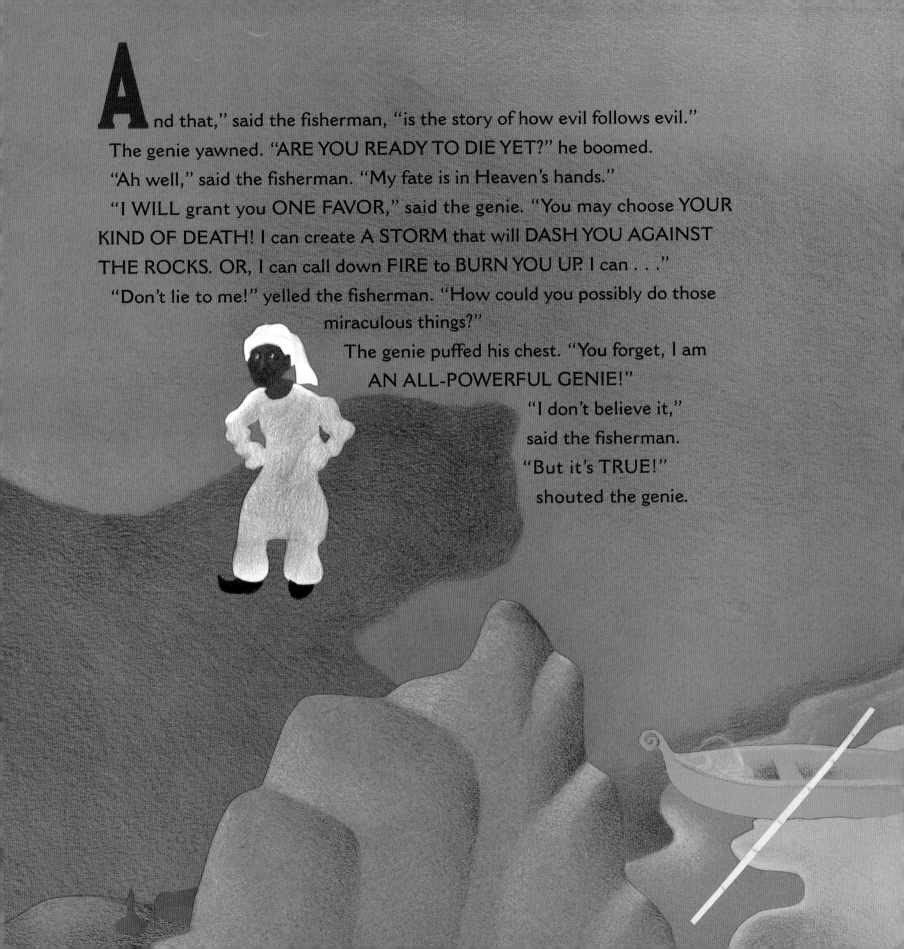

And that," said the fisherman, "is the story of how evil follows evil."

The genie yawned. "ARE YOU READY TO DIE YET?" he boomed.

"Ah well," said the fisherman. "My fate is in Heaven's hands."

"I WILL grant you ONE FAVOR," said the genie. "You may choose YOUR KIND OF DEATH! I can create A STORM that will DASH YOU AGAINST THE ROCKS. OR, I can call down FIRE to BURN YOU UP. I can . . ."

"Don't lie to me!" yelled the fisherman. "How could you possibly do those miraculous things?"

The genie puffed his chest. "You forget, I am AN ALL-POWERFUL GENIE!"

"I don't believe it," said the fisherman. "But it's TRUE!" shouted the genie.

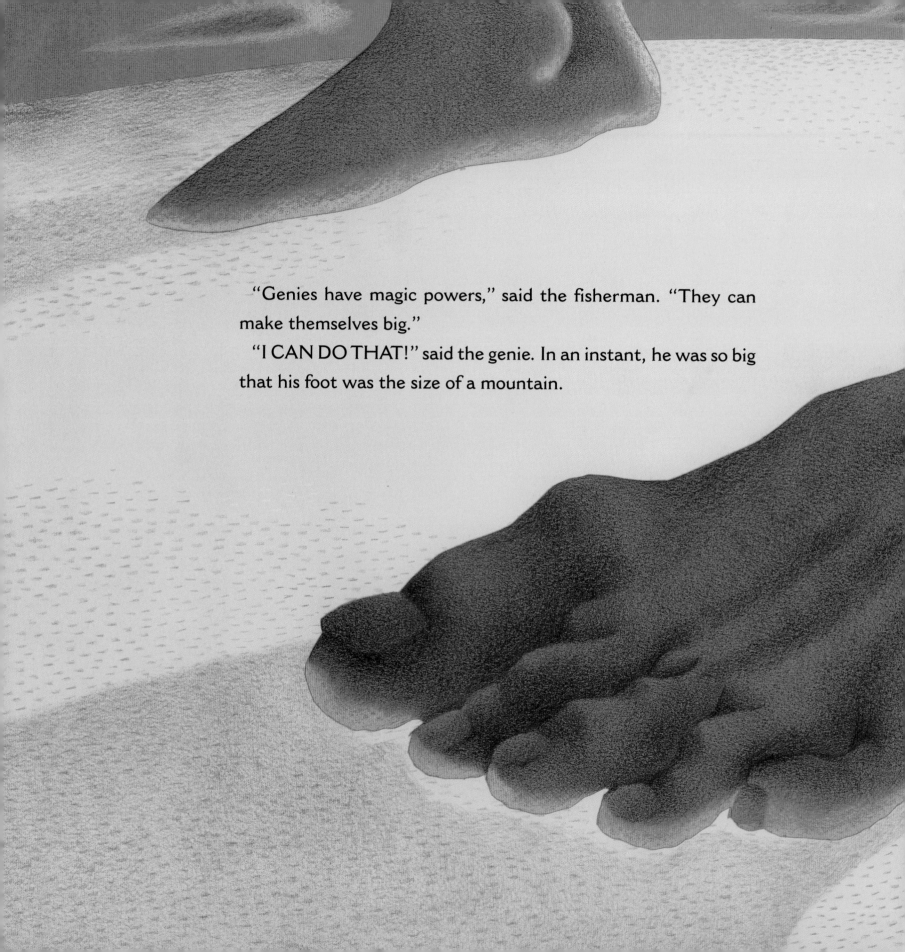

"Genies have magic powers," said the fisherman. "They can make themselves big."

"I CAN DO THAT!" said the genie. In an instant, he was so big that his foot was the size of a mountain.

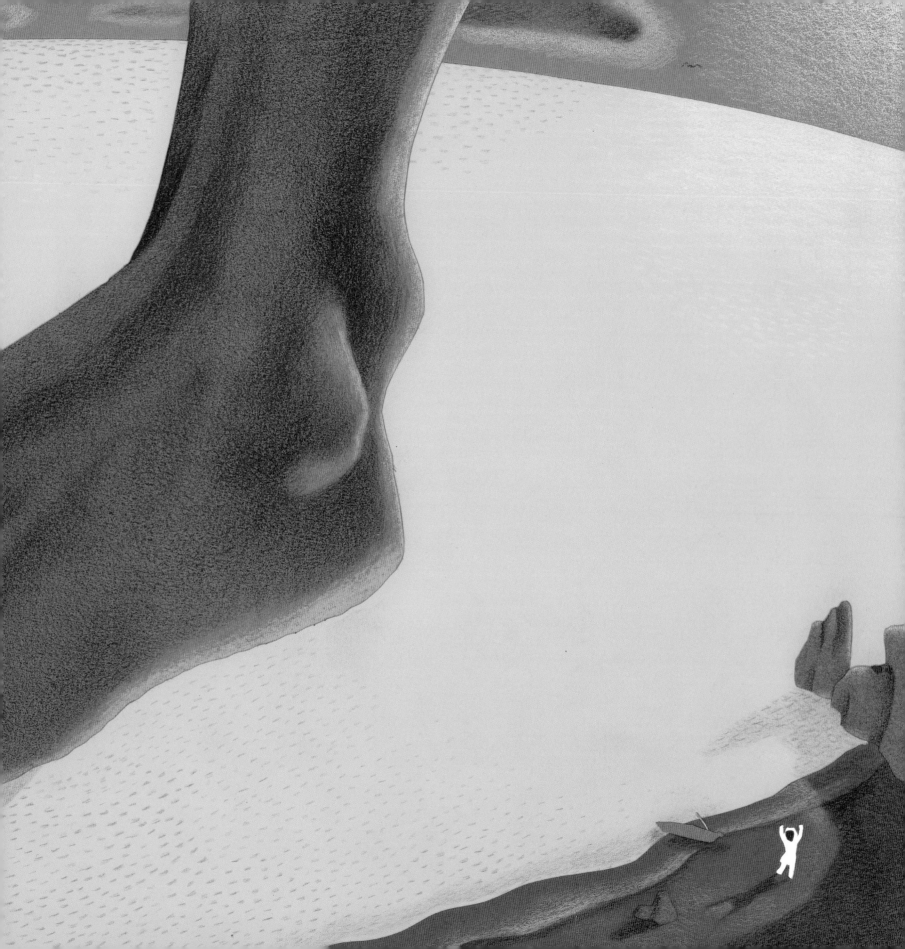

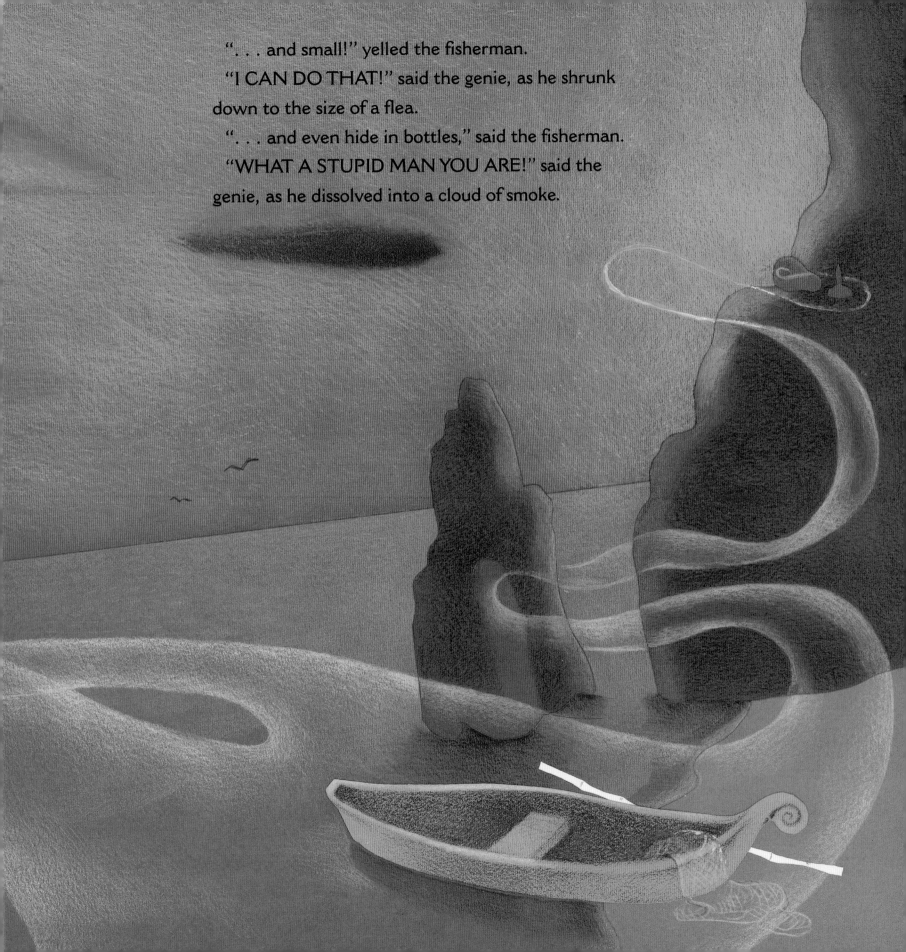

". . . and small!" yelled the fisherman.

"I CAN DO THAT!" said the genie, as he shrunk
down to the size of a flea.

". . . and even hide in bottles," said the fisherman.

"WHAT A STUPID MAN YOU ARE!" said the
genie, as he dissolved into a cloud of smoke.

The smoke swirled around like a tornado, and funneled itself back into the bottle.

And the fisherman picked up the bottle, shoved the cork into it, and threw it, as hard as he could, out to sea.

The rising of the moon.
The setting of the sun.
The teller is tired.
The story is done.

DISCARDED